ANSIBLE

Season One

Stant Litore

FICTION BY STANT LITORE

THE ZOMBIE BIBLE

Death Has Come Up into Our Windows
What Our Eyes Have Witnessed
Strangers in the Land
No Lasting Burial
I Will Hold My Death Close
By a Slender Thread (forthcoming)

THE ANSIBLE STORIES

Ansible: Season One
Ansible 15718

and

The Running of the Tyrannosaurs

Dante's Heart

The Dark Need (The Dead Man, #20)
with Lee Goldberg and William Rabkin

ANSIBLE

SEASON ONE

ANSIBLE 15715

ANSIBLE 15716

ANSIBLE 15717

ANSIBLE 2

STANT LITORE

Westmarch Publishing

2015

Text copyright © 2015 Daniel Fusch.

Stant Litore is a pen name for Daniel Fusch.

Cover art by Roberto Calas.

ISBN: 978-1-942458-06-7

A Westmarch Publishing release.

Contact Stant Litore:
www.stantlitore.com
zombiebible@gmail.com
www.facebook.com/stant.litore
@thezombiebible

CONTENTS

for Jessica

ANSIBLE 15715

Please hear me. We are all in danger, the most terrible danger; we are all going to die terrible deaths. If you can hear me, if anyone can hear me, remember these words. Please. Pass them on to your children, and to theirs. You are our one hope.

I gaze out at all of your faces, so full of lust to hear my screams, and I weep as the wood is stacked about my feet. I am mad to think that any of you are psi-capable, that any of you can hear even a word, even a single word from my mind. Oh Allah, Allah, I am begging you, if any of you can hear me!

I am Ansible 15715, and I was born Malala Ali, named for a hero of my people, a woman who fought to save minds. I was born in the year 2419 by your calendar, and in the year 2444 I graduated with multiple degrees in linguistics and psionics from KAUST, a university that does not yet exist. I was so, so hopeful, so wild with joy when I was named for the Starmind project. Allah forgive me for what I have done.

***

There were four of us initially, but mine was the only mind to survive the transfer. That was the first terror; if only it had been the last! I opened my eyes on what I assumed was an alien world, saw no sky above me but a darkness of rock, and pale lights around me from bioluminescent, stationary creatures that grew on the walls of that cavern. I got up on one elbow as quickly as I could, and there were three others there with me. Two were dead. The third— her eyes were rolling and she was babbling monosyllables and drooling.

I remember my heart pounding. I remember leaping up, screaming, then screaming again because my voice was so deep and raw. The body I had transferred to was so *different*. Human, clearly, but different; I stumbled, not knowing at first how to keep balance. I was naked and this body was obviously male, and it had so little muscle. On earth I had trained until I could do a decathlon; it had been a source of pride for me in college. Starmind had reinforced this. "A sound mind in a sound body": that had been one of their mottoes, one that I agreed with, though I thought it a strange choice for Starmind, a slogan borrowed from another continent and another time.

Now I was here, in a body sluggish and barely responsive, in an anatomy and chemistry alien to me. I tried to breathe deeply and calmly, and walk through the steps I'd been trained for. I checked my fellow survivor's vitals and was dismayed to find her heartbeat was unsteady; even as my fingers measured her pulse, her lips stopped moving and her silence carried her into sleep or coma. Shaking, I shut my eyes and looked inside, into the dark. Calling out, again and again, in my mind.

There was no answer.

I must have called fifty or sixty times, with intervals between for quiet, intense listening.

I opened my eyes, stared bleakly at the faces of my dead companions, faces I didn't know but which had, for the brief seconds of our arrival, concealed behind them the minds of men and women I had trained with, competed with, and loved. The woman's breast stopped moving as I watched; she died as silently as water dies in the desert. I closed her eyes with my fingers. My hands shook as I stood.

I gazed out at the rocky contours of this world, so many light years from home, a world without a sky. I called out once more inside myself and still was greeted with silence.

And then I knew.

The mind that had inhabited this atrophied, male body had not survived my transfer into it. I was alone.

Whoever this man had been, I had killed him.

***

I shiver now, thinking of that world. Its horrors are more vivid to me than this kindling the guards are packing about my feet. I saw...Allah, the things that I *saw*. A cavern large enough to hold five minsters the size of the one here on your hill, a cavern where a vast herd, *vast*, of naked humans walked stooped over, grazing on the bioluminescent worms that live everywhere on the rock, plucking the small lives like berries and lifting them to their mouths. Upside-down forests of stalactites hanging from the high stone roof threw back an eerie glow from the biolight of the grubs the humans fed on. But the most terrible thing was the *eyes* of these humans. Dead eyes. Eyes with no spark of mind behind them. I guessed, right or wrong, that it was the worms that drugged them so, wresting their reason and intellect from them, their passion for life, reducing them to slow-moving, cud-chewing cattle. So I did not touch the worms myself, though hunger tore at my belly as though I had caged rats in there and they were trying to eat their way out of me. I would sit alone with a rock wall to my back, hugging myself in my arms and shaking, my hunger raw within me, my phallus flaccid and cold in the cave air. I suffered fiercely, but I think my guess was right. Later, I saw that the masters of these herds, when it came time for slaughter, isolated their prey and deprived them of food. I saw a woman in a small cave that served as a pen, watched her quietly as the hours passed unmarked and unknown. There were worms in the walls behind me, but no worms within her small prison; she sat in the dark. After a long time, she began to whimper. I saw her eyes shine like cat's eyes in the lights from the worms that she could not reach or touch. I could see her only faintly, but I *heard* the life return to her with the onset of hunger. Heard her babbling in the dark. Finally, she caught sight of me, and when I saw the way she shrank back, her eyes wide with terror, I fled. My heart pounding. Her terror unsettled me, nearly panicked me. All my life I had been subject to the hungering glances of men, to the fear of being grabbed on some night walk, of being bruised and torn, used as though I were only a thing, and a thing owned by someone else, not by me. It had almost happened once. And at times I had seen the fear of that in another woman's eyes. But I had never seen anyone look at *me* with that fear.

At last, I couldn't bear it. I curled into a ball in a dark corner where no worms were, and shook until the horror of it had passed. My phallus lay limp against my leg and it was alien to me, so alien.

***

I think I wept; in any case, when I woke, my face was damp. I woke hating myself for my fear. I had not known what I would find when I became an Ansible, but I had known that it might be fearful. I had not expected, *could not* have expected such a nightmare as this, but I was a woman of an ancient family and a graduate of KAUST, the finest research institution on the planet. It was shameful that I should crawl weeping into the dark. Yet I did not know how to manage this body's reactions; its hormones were strange to me. Some times I wanted to scream and drive my fist or my forehead into the walls; sometimes I wanted to remain in a fetal position for days. It is even possible that I did; I had no way of knowing time, except by the extremity of my hunger.

At last I stood shakily and walked with quiet steps back to the woman's cave. I meant to speak to her, I think, or to project to her psionically, to apologize for frightening her, and to listen if she needed me to. I had an instinct to reach out to her as to a sister. She would not have understood my Arabic or my Farsi, but for some reason this didn't occur to me then. The sudden need to be there for her, for another human being whose eyes had a mind behind them, was overwhelming. I found that I was running.

But when I reached her cave, it was empty and the bars across the entrance were gone. I plucked a biolight from the wall and crawled inside, hardly daring to breathe. In the glow from my hand, I expected to see a dark smear across the interior wall, but there was none. My nostrils flared, but I could smell no blood. There were feces in one corner—I smelled *those*—but otherwise no physical sign that a woman had ever been here. Yet—I could almost *hear* her, shrieking, screaming until her throat went raw. I strained my ears, but it was like something scraping across the edge of my mind. Such terrible screams. I shivered and backed out of her emptied cell.

***

My hunger continued to rip at my belly, and I found myself sleeping unexpectedly, fitfully, and often. When I thought to, I knelt for prayers. I had to guess at the hours. There was no time in that eternal dark, no change in the biolights on the walls. And I had to guess at what direction to kneel in. Should I look at the stone roof, assuming earth—and Mecca—to be up there? That did not seem right. I developed the custom of turning to the right to pray, each time. I supposed consistency would be most respectful to Allah.

Once, I tried to accost one of the cud-chewers, a male roughly my own size, his limbs nearly atrophied from little use, his only exercise consisting of slow grazing. This man had a mind, at least a rudimentary one; the clarity I had seen in the woman's eyes, in her cell, made that clear to me. It was only the worms that drugged him. I could not empty his belly for him; I had no way to bind him or imprison him for the time it would take to starve him, and even if I did, I would probably perish while I waited. Already I could feel my ribs standing out grotesquely against my skin. I kept running my left hand along them, feeling their hard, brittle ridges and the low valleys of my skin between them.

No, I couldn't starve this man. But surely I could say something, do *something*, to make him glance about at the herd with clearer eyes. If I could only find someone to talk to, to pray with, someone to share my horror, my dread— if only I could do *that*, I could—I don't know—I could think, at least a little, of resistance. I could *hope*, I could feel something other than terror. I thought it safer to approach a male with this experiment in mind; the one woman I had met whose mind had cleared had found *me* an object of terror. Perhaps if I could wake this man, it would be different.

I crouched beside him, but he didn't appear to notice me. He reached right past my shoulder to pluck a grub from the wall. His movements were slow, as though he were sleepwalking. I struck his arm, feebly, but he didn't react. I gripped his shoulder. Still no reaction. I tried standing between him and the next grub within reach, but he only stared vacantly at my chest a moment, not even seeking out my eyes. Then he shambled around me, nudging me absently out of his way as he reached behind my back. I shrank from the touch; he unnerved me.

Taking a breath, I tried psi. Touching most minds is like dipping your hand in warm water, and thoughts native to that mind either rise from the deep like fish to nibble gently at your fingers, or they don't. Most minds never know your hand is there. But touching this man's mind was like touching the slimy skin of a slug; it resisted entry and it repulsed me. I shuddered and tried speech instead. But my Arabic sounded strangely slurred through lips I wasn't used to. Nor did it make any difference. And with a start, and a glance about me at the silent herd shuffling along between dark pillars of rock, I realized that it was entirely possible that none of these humans *had ever heard speech.*

How could they? If they spent all their lives like this?

Yet how were they *born*? How did they mate? I saw no children here. In horror, I imagined great vats where these humans were grown, before being loosed fully adult in these caverns. Or worse, some nursery deep within this world where sentient women raised their young—perhaps even teaching them to think and speak!—until, at some prescribed age, at puberty perhaps, their children were torn from them, robbed of their minds, and sent to this hell.

I had no way to know which of these visions was true, or if either was. I still don't know.

***

I followed the herd for a while, sometimes broadcasting in psi—which should have felt like scattering pebbles over a lake and listening for the splashes, but instead felt like setting my hand lightly on a swarming mass of slugs or naked snails—and at last I stopped, unable to bear it. I tried thinking of some other strategy for waking them—or, at least, one of them. Their hundreds scared me. I hadn't been good at handling that many people even on our own planet. The thought of having to address such a great crowd was a nightmare itself. Also, my failed experiment with the vacant-faced male haunted me; I found I couldn't muster the courage for a second, more intimate try, one mind touching one other. So I watched them, and trailed them, and when the sight of them all *eating* became too much for me, I ducked aside between the stalagmites and searched out small pools of cave water, which was clear and cool in my cupped hands—nothing like the still, processed water of the planet I had known. It was the one good thing in this place.

Starmind never told me what to expect here; they probably hadn't known. They said only that their most finely tuned psionic instruments had detected other minds, human minds, sentient minds, though silent ones— somewhere out there, in space. We asked so many questions at first, but soon learned not to; Starmind was not KAUST. We were told what to do and we did it. That was the price of our admission to the first contact program. We were told only that we would leap across the void from body to body—a poetic way to describe it, and not really accurate. A copy of our minds would be placed in those foreign bodies, out there. This was a scary but exciting thing; our ansible technology is still so rudimentary, still so new. Starmind believed the leap would burn out our original bodies, scorch the original mind, so they would not be able to read our experience; once on this world, we would be autonomous. They must have judged it worth the risk. Later, there might be teams advanced enough to maintain an active link with our homeworld. But we were to be the first. We were to contact the other humans and let them know they were not alone among the stars. *Salaam*, we were to say.

We knew we weren't coming back.

I don't know what I expected. A city, probably, maybe one with alien lines to its architecture and even an alien sun to power its glass panels. But a city of thriving human beings, of minds engaged in study or in loving or in politics, as human minds are engaged all over our own world.

Not this.

***

To keep panic at bay, I began to explore the physical space of this enclosed world, marking the spot where I began by scratching the wall with my nails. I found that I could make a circuit of the entire cavern between one sleep and the next. I found only a single egress, a dark opening about three meters across. I touched the walls inside it and found them worn smooth, but I could do nothing more, because even standing near it, let alone touching it, brought me pangs of terror, my breast constricting. After backing away, I had to lean against a rock pillar and breathe, *breathe*, pain throughout the left side of my body. I don't know for how long; afterward, I was very tired, and went to find some place far away from that opening where I might curl up with my back to a wall and sleep.

***

By then, my reason was at risk: the hunger of this strange body I wore made it all but impossible to form coherent thoughts. Several times, I caught myself wandering without direction across the cavern; I wandered in the same way inside my mind. At times I just clutched at my ears and wept, feeling that I was no longer even human, just an animal, just a mute, hungering thing. Often as I sat huddled, the silent herd passed, grazing all around me, naked and fat, and none of them even glanced at me. Often I prayed that it would just end. I had no way to end it myself.

***

And now I have to tell you the terrible part, the part that you must hear, that someone *must* hear, before you burn me! Yet how can I make you understand? You mustn't think of an invasion of armored soldiers that your own might repel. These *cannot* be repelled. Please. You have to share my terror. You have to.

I will try to describe the creatures, the keepers of that herd, the beings that issued from that dark opening in the wall. Only, I don't know how that will help. You will never see them.

They were large, much larger than human beings. They walk cloaked in shadow; if you look directly at them, you can hardly see them, though you can *feel* them there, like something terrible and violent that might eviscerate you and rape you, and you want to run, run as fast as you can, only you can't take your gaze from them. You just stand still, hesitating, shaking. Then they close on you. You feel their appendages, hundreds of them, like threads of silk. At first there is no pain; but at their touch, your *fear* becomes more intense than anything you have ever felt, anything you have ever *imagined* feeling.

I had made a habit of returning to the woman's cell, to that cold place where the walls were dark. I would stand there without any light and listen to her shrieks in my mind for as long as I could bear it. I thought that maybe I would understand what had happened to her, what this place was, why humans were kept here like this. But always, in the end, I had to scurry from that cell before I began shrieking myself, and the last time I did, *they* caught me.

They were waiting there. Just outside.

It was as if they had known all about me: my

emaciation; the sharp, fast-induced clarity of my mind; my frequent pilgrimages to this cell.

I tried to plead with them as they came at me, and I sent my thoughts at them, louder than I ever had before. I ducked back into that cell, that horrible place where the other woman had died. With my back naked against the cold wall, I lifted my fists. I was wearing a man's body; in my horror, all language having failed me, I tried a man's response, one body's aggression against another. I struck at them. Vaguely, I remember skin tearing like paper at my blows. A thin, ripping sound. But no noise of pain, no outcry.

Then they surrounded me, and I was blind and cold in the dark. Hundreds of silk threads caressed my skin, and though I tried to swing my fists, they no longer moved. I could hear their minds, like whispers all around me. Suddenly one of them was *loud*. I rang with its voice like a glass struck by a fork; I think I cried out, but I couldn't hear my own cry.

Eight billion, it said. *Eight billion cattle. You would have hid this from us, little mind? Eight billion—the means for our species to go on existing? And a world with atmosphere, ideal for raising large herds. There is so much information in your mind. Constellations that can be seen from your sky, distances in light years from interstellar landmarks. We can pinpoint the exact location of your planet. We could move our bodies there, but we do not even need to. We have your psi imprint. We can find others like it. We can send our own minds there, make new bodies for ourselves, and feed, and feed. And you, little mind, would have hid this from us!*

Then the voice faded, and I fell, and fell. Through endless dark. And there were teeth and needles all around me, so many punctures, so much pain and terror. I screamed and screamed…

***

I don't know how long. When I woke, I lay on a bed, and those creatures were gathered all around me, clicking and waving their cilia like kelp in the sea. And from the whiteness of the walls I knew that we were in my mind, this bed was in my mind. I recognized this place; it was the psychiatric ward at First Psionic Medical in Medina. I visited there for my postgraduate research, studied the patients. Even tried to speak into some of their minds, in a very careful way.

So I knew we were *in* my mind.

That scared me.

They were in my mind. Those things.

Not just their voices, not just their thoughts. More of their being than that. Like a transfer. Except my mind was still alive, and they were all in there with me!

I screamed and thrashed my head, but I couldn't move my body. I tried to think of another place, other people, but I couldn't change anything. Those walls, the bed beneath me, my own body—all of it stayed fixed in place. *They* had forced me open, and they were in control.

I think for a while, I lost my sanity.

I wept and begged and screamed incoherently.

And at last their voices came at me, and my mind's thrashing stopped; I was like an insect pinned to a board.

Why feed on you like this, they said, *when there are eight billion on which to feed? For what you have hidden from us, you will suffer otherwise. We will deprive ourselves of one meal.*

We have found your planet, as we said we would.

We will release your mind, let it return there.

You can try to warn them. They will not believe you. We have seen this. You will suffer and beg and they will not believe you, they will not even hear you. And even if they did, what could they do? They are cattle, and we will feed.

They will not hear you.

***

In the next instant, I woke here, in this body, female, white-skinned, pale hair. So young. Her name was Mary, and I am truly sorry for the death of her mind.

I have tried to tell the others in the house with me. I have tried to tell the bishop in the minster. I have tried, I have tried. I tried to leave messages on parchment. I tried to carve one into the wall of a church. Oh Allah, I have tried. This is my last hope, our last hope.

It is all too clear what has happened; it was unexpected, but I could write a paper on it if I were home, and not about to die here. When Starmind transferred me from KAUST to that *hell*, I was sent forward in time, not just across space. And when those creatures flung me back, I was flung *back* across time, also. It is like a recoil, except it has flung me further back than my point of origin. Too far back. That is what they meant.

They intend to leap forward as I did, coming to their planet. They will arrive on earth at some point *after* the moment of my original transfer in the year 2447, some moment after my undated arrival on their world. Maybe they will arrive a few years after that, maybe a few minutes, maybe a few centuries. I don't know. They clearly are better at this than we.

***

You are burning me because the bishop says I speak to devils and relay visions of hell. The armored men approach the wood about my feet with torches, oh Allah, with *torches*, even now. I am begging you to hear me. Someone in the crowd, someone watching from a window. If you can hear these words in your mind, if you can hear even a whisper, *I am the girl below, tied to the stake.* You *must* hear me. You must remember! Someone must tell the president of the Starmind project. Please! I am Ansible 15715. In the year 2444, or 2445, or 2446, one of your descendants must tell the president of Starmind that you have a message from Ansible 15715. You must tell him *not* to send. *Not* to send. You must tell him. You must. I am Ansible 15715. Remember!

***

The creatures—they are pneumavores. Do you understand? They eat the minds, the souls, of their prey. A biologist could explain it better; early in their evolution they must have been some kind of leech. Nature selected those with more aggressive psi talent, those that could inflict some horror on the minds they were ingesting. The pneumavores I encountered on that planet were terribly adept. They trapped their victims in nightmares, nightmares that could go on almost forever, because in a nightmare you can live a thousand years in a single minute of waking time. That is a lot of fear to eat, a lot of psionic activity if a creature feeds on that.

And they are coming *here*.

To do *that*—to all of us. *To all of your children*, so many years from now.

But that is not what scares me most.

I *am* scared, so scared. Because I may not truly be tied to this stake.

I may not be on earth.

They may *still* be feeding on me.

When this fire consumes me, or when I asphyxiate, I may only slip into some fresh nightmare, a terrible afterlife within my mind. I don't know. I can't know. The fire—oh Allah, Allah, the fire licks at my feet! Oh God!—Oh God! If you can hear me, anyone, if you can hear me, oh, if you are real, if this fire is real, please listen. Please remember. Please tell them. Please. Allah, I burn! I burn!

ANSIBLE 15716

This will be my last final broadcast. I know I said that yesterday, and the day before, and all the days before that after climbing this salt ridge and lifting my whiskers to the stars. But this must be, truly, the last. There is no more time. I am dying.

***

Twenty years before Starmind sent me out here, I went on the hajj, so I know about journeys and their endings. And I know about being lost in the desert on the way.

Being a fool and a youth then, I wandered from the road, just my camel and I, to pick a purple flower I saw growing from the face of a dune. Then wind swept up, and even as I started back, blossom and stalk cupped in my hand, the air fell like a veil across my way, and it was full of sand and grit, like tiny specks of glass—cutting at my skin, they blew so fast. The sound the air made was obscene, like tearing metal. I slid from my saddle and took shelter behind my camel, whose anxious voice I could hardly hear above the screech of the sky.

I had not considered that I might not make it to Mecca.

I thought of many things as the wind tore away the world. My wife's face. The classes I was taking at KAUST, the other students. The muezzin and the prayers at dawn. I called out into the wind at last, unable to bear it. Allah, I called. Allah, Allah. We are told that he is a God of deserts. No doubt here, more than in the bright cities, he must hear me.

But there came no answer. Only the shattering sand.

And that went on a long time.

***

At last I woke with a start, parched and shaken. I was half entombed in sand, but the air on my face was still. Glancing up, I could see stars blazing hot and terrifying, far brighter than any I had seen before. And I realized that though I might pray to him and revere him, Allah might not hear me, not in that vastness of dark with who knows how many billions of burning suns. With all the universe around me and only gravity and a thin coat of sand holding me to this pebble spinning within it, without roof or walls to give me the illusion of my own security and importance, for the first time I felt disconnected. Tentative. Provisional.

I yearned then for Allah as I have never yearned before, not even for a woman.

But there was only the sand and the stars scattered like sand, the flower dead in my palm. And the warmth of the camel at my back, my only connection with another living thing.

Connection.

Contact.

We long for that, all our lives, no matter who we are. I understood that, gazing at the stars that night. And I understood it more terribly when I first arrived here.

***

The transfer of an intelligence from one body to another across the void is a wrenching, annihilatory experience. One moment, my eyes were open on a garden at the Starmind facility, and I could hear the humming of small birds with fast, flickering wings, imported from the Americas. Then a sensation like being caught in a collision, and I opened my eyes again though I had not closed them. At first I panicked. All around me there was blinding whiteness under a desert sun, and the quiet breathing of strange creatures I had never seen before.

Leaping up, I realized that I was one of them. My training returned to me and I called to the others, hoping my colleagues were there with me. But while the minds I touched were porous and soft, none of them responded— as though I were peering through windows into houses whose inhabitants had secreted themselves into inner rooms, as my ancestors secreted their wives. No one drew aside any curtain or veil at my call. To this day I do not know if that was because the other members of my Ansible team were not there or because of some limitation inherent to this body's neurology. Maybe I *cannot* reach others with psi, and others cannot reach me. I hope that's not true.

I tried communicating by physical means, but I was clumsy at this, and it was only by the hooting and the singing of the others that I realized my thighbones were perforated and so constructed that I could blow air through them and make sound. And I did, but no doubt I sounded like a tuba out of tune, nothing like the high fluting voices I heard around me. The others, some twenty in number, fell silent and listened as I swayed awkwardly on my six long legs and tried in vain to imitate the sounds I'd heard them make. What a confusion I must have been, to them no less than to myself.

I gazed at their dark eyes, which were moist like horses' eyes, and could not tell who was gazing back. I turned my head, startling myself at how quickly my neck moved. All around me, the whiteness of salt, and a sky lighter than any I had known, terrifying in its lightness, as though I might fall up and tumble into the fire of that younger sun. I bleated like an animal, lost and alone. After a moment, the others bleated with me, imitating *my* sounds. Yet I felt no less alone, no less abandoned. I remembered the solitude in the desert on my hajj. This place is like that. So vast, it makes the mind a desert, too.

***

This last psicast is my report, though I can't know if my mind is even transmitting. Starmind searches the universe for other sentient minds, but we know so little of the bodies that produce them, of what they are capable or not. Still, if there is even a chance this report can be heard, I must try to make it useful.

These are the facts I know about the world to which Starmind has sent me. The planet, or at least this part of it, is covered in salt that might be a hundred meters deep. The salt has been shaped by unknown processes into high, spectacular ridges, and in some places into pillars and tall white towers. The people here—yes, I call them people— have hollowed out the towers, and after mating, they gestate their young inside. The towers remind me of the homes that ancient tribes carved in the cliffs of our own Mount Aktepe, back home. Except that these towers stand out alone, or two and three together, like men on their way to Mecca, clothed in white, crossing the sand.

The people here are beautifully adapted to a life of salt. They can drink the dead pools, their bodies straining the salt from the water after ingestion. Each of their six limbs end in long fingers of bone, many-jointed. These fingers are capable of digging into the salt to a depth of thirty centimeters, or so I estimate. The people can cling in this way, upside-down, to the bottom of a salt shelf, for days, even years. I don't know what instinct they obey or what purpose, but I have seen them. I have seen the red of the sun in their hair and heard their warbling notes in the silence at dusk.

There isn't much life here, not really. Microbes cling to the salt and feed several species of tiny crawlers, which the people lick up with slender, adhesive tongues. A few bright-plumaged insects and the people themselves, complex organisms, must be the last survivals of some environmental cataclysm, some extinction that left only a few hardy species behind. In this salt desert, as on the Sahara, the few signs of a biology beyond that of mere sediment are to be cherished. They are like touches of Allah's hand, who paints brightly though sparingly.

The people have long, stiltlike legs, but these appear to be vestigial, pre-extinction-event, as the people are neither migratory nor nomadic. I am grateful for these legs, however; they have been a great help in my own explorations.

***

I can travel far in a day. Perhaps a hundred kilometers; it is impossible to know precisely. Before I sent my first final broadcast, I tried once to reach the edge of the desert, to verify whether the desert *had* edges. A few of the others followed me for a time, keening in their high voices, my mate especially. I think they mourned my departure, which surely they could not understand or justify. Their song of loss affected me deeply, though I could not answer it; I have their instruments of speech, the same whistling holes and flute holes in my thighs, but I haven't their language. Had my body been human, I might have wept.

As it was, I just loped swiftly across the ridges and waves of salt, leaving them far behind. Perhaps forever: I live now with a tribe of such creatures, having made my way back, but though these have the same markings on their flanks, and one of them the same, or a similar, limp, I can't be sure—can't be *entirely* sure—that this is the *same* tribe.

There was wind in my eyes, out there, and the white knife of the sun's glare; secondary and then tertiary eyelids slid closed, surprising me as I gazed through them as through a woman's veil. I hadn't known I had such eyelids, until that moment.

I did not rest by day or by dark. I did not know my body's limits, any more than I knew the limits of the desert. I was desperate in my solitude, and desperate in my yearning for the other living things that I had left, and anxious to find something that would be more familiar, and a comfort. Perhaps the minds of the other Ansibles who had been supposed to arrive with me; perhaps they had been cast into bodies far elsewhere on this planet. Perhaps I could still find them. Or even if I could find a green field, or a lake abundant with fish, or a pomegranate tree: meeting one of those would have been like meeting a human face.

But all the time that I have been here, I have seen nothing green. On that journey, I saw only silent, ghostly formations of salt, some like small mountains, as though some immense beast stranded by a vanished ecology had breathed its last or some ship had plummeted into the world only to be concealed by centuries of salt. In the end, I stopped and just gazed at one of those white mountains, as though in prayer. As I contemplated that eternity of salt, the world turned, embracing and then rejecting the sun, again and again. At last, my body's need for water—though less sharp than a human's—stirred me. In a kind of quiet despair, I glanced at the horizon, at far shapes that were not forests or cities but only other, stranger saline forms, looming like giants on the edges of dreams.

I do not think those mountains were sunken beasts or buried ships, travelers stranded here as I was. I think that if I had hands and a pickax and were to dig through them, I would find only minute white crystals, all the way through. I have thought, sometimes, of my ancestors, how they labored under a hard sun for bricks of salt, and what a paradise of wealth they would have found here, on this dead, beautiful world.

**

It took me a long time to return, though I traveled fast; having found no mythical edge to this desert, I fled my failure with a holy terror. Also, I was frightened of what might happen if I didn't find the people I had met here at first; I was scared of being lost, alone out here, forever. I think for a while I was mad.

I drove myself hard. It is possible no other member of this species ever ran as fast as I did across those salt slopes. Devoid of natural predators or of any religious instinct for pilgrimage, they would see no need of haste. In retrospect, it is a surprise that my stiltlike legs did not crack from the strain. Small wisps of salt crystals filled the air behind me like a flock of fragile and momentary angels, torn up by my long fingers as I ran.

At last I loped along the last ridge and saw white towers below me, dotting the salt valley like magnificent artworks bereft of a creator, and the pools of salt water, dead and empty but for the petrified remnants of ancient and no longer extant beings, yet beautiful in their death as they threw back the glare of the sun. Those pools blinded me for a moment as the salt expanse hadn't. In a moment of stark clarity I recalled the face of my first wife, back on earth, the first time she had lifted her veil: how her face had shone in the sunlight. How I had gasped at her newness and beauty; I'd been plunged breathless into a world made suddenly strange yet infinitely more real than the one in which I'd stood until that moment.

I trotted past the pools, and a few people came out from between the towers and approached me. One faster than the rest: my mate. She reached me, drove her flank into me, and we leaned into each other. She twined her neck about mine and her whiskers were a dry scratch along my cheek. Then, in the thrill of the heat and movement of our bodies I thought of nothing else.

Until afterward.

I woke from the haze after mating with a shock, and I found her dark eye a mere breath from my own. Again I was standing in an alien body on an alien world, and though her body was warm against mine and her eye was beautiful, it was beautiful the way an agate is beautiful, or the surface of a garden pond. It glinted with a promise of life and soul, but I could not know whose. I had answered the demands of my body, which were fiercer and more primal than any I had felt before transferring into it, but now part of me wanted to turn and bolt back into the desert, flee her and flee all these unknowable people.

Most terrifying was the sudden thought that my mate's body might, or might not, hold silent within it the mind of one of my lost colleagues, one of the other two Ansibles who had transferred with me, one of whom had been a man and one a woman. Yet even if one of them inhabited my mate, she—or he—might not know that *I* was within *this* body. He—or she—might think of *me* as only one of these indigenes, might have drawn near me not out of recognition but only in response to the urgent, hormonal necessities of these new bodies in which we lived.

But this might be only a fantasy. I could see nothing in her eyes. Perhaps the other members of Ansible 15716 were lost. I had tried once, on this planet, to scratch Arabic letters in the salt with my fingers, to signal the others, but I found I could not remember how to make them. Then I had drawn patterns in the sand, any pattern I could, while the others watched me impassively. None responded. Surely this meant I was alone, though it might have meant only that the other members of my team, their minds bent perhaps even more than my own by this new biology, had not recognized what I was doing; it was despair at that uncertainty that drove me out into the wastes.

I could not even be sure that my mate was the same with whom I had been before my hajj across the salt. She pressed herself to me in the same way, and she was missing one whisker on the left of her long face, as my mate had been missing one before my departure, but that was small evidence. How many of these people might lose a whisker? She might be another entirely. This might even be another valley entirely. How could I know?

I began shaking, and she made soft, warbling sounds—whether to calm me or question me, I don't know. It was a long time before I stopped trembling.

***

I have only a vague sense of what drove me to Starmind. They wanted anthropologists, I know, and in this dying discipline I was one of the names people knew. Starmind's recruiters had already reached their tentacles into my life for many years, but mostly I had closed the door on them, severing one or two slimy appendages between door and jamb if I could. I had two wives, one of whom remained a delight in bed, and a lucrative career; there was nothing to drive me out into the empty spaces between the stars.

I think that changed for me the night of the Perseids. My second wife and I took our glider up into the hills, having secured a permit for leaving the city, and when we were far from the urban dome of light pollution, we found the stars unbearably bright, as though someone had switched on the sky. We watched the meteors flash and burn, and I kissed my wife and made love to her on a shelf of rock that still bore some of the day's heat. Our love was frantic and desperate; I think I was trying to drown out the distant roar of those burning suns with our gasps and moans, trying as she enclosed me in her warmth to forget the cold of the dark spaces between them.

It was no good. I had gazed up at those violent stars too many times during the hajj, and this night brought back all my unease from that time. When I lay later with my lover in my arms, exhausted, sweaty, and sated, those thoughts pressed on me again. Yes, I had a passionate wife, and another, comfortable one. Yes, I had a post at KAUST, a university ancient and prestigious. I even had the honorific after my name to show that I had fulfilled my duty to Allah and completed the hajj. Yet I felt emptied out. I had not done enough with my short life. Not when our world spun light-choked and slowly dying under such a vastness of stars. I was aware of how small we were and how immense Allah's universe was; surely I, and everyone else too, was meant to do more than just live and love and breed. The words of Mohammad that I had read so often as a child and recited so often at prayers came back to me and they burned in the dark with a clarity they had never owned before, not even when I stood at the black rock at Mecca: we were to be emissaries, riding out always across the desert spaces, carrying the word of the Prophet and his longing for union—even for union between all those points of light, to bind each discrete moment in the universe to each other, and rob even that multiplicity of alien suns of its terror.

My wife must have sensed something of my strange thoughts, for she kissed me and drew me into her again, but though our second loving that night was no less passionate, it was even less successful at making me forget the long scream of meteors dying by fire above our heated bodies. We make roofs that capture the light of the sun to heat and brighten our homes, and we live surrounded by millions of such roofs so that we exist without ever seeing the stars. Yet how can we forget? How can we possibly forget?

In the morning, I called the president of Starmind, bypassing the recruiters entirely. I had measured well in the standard tests of psionic ability, but the training program, I knew, could take years. There was no use delaying.

***

There are nights on this planet that have a silence unknown on earth, not even in the Sahara or the Rub' al Khali, where the wind at least is restless. Sometimes here there is no wind, and if I stand far from the others where I cannot hear their breathing, the silence becomes thunder. At first this was frightening. Then I learned that when I stand in it, the silence can beat into nonexistence my memories, my fears, my doubts, so that I become a mere natural thing, merely breathing. There is a certain peace in being a natural thing, a part of the desert, a rock or a tree or a silent person. Without violence or desire.

This body has no chemical defense against insanity, and for a while I preserved myself by postponing all memory of where I had been or where I had come from. I lived and sweated and mated as many organisms have done since the worlds first formed out of the ashes of stars. That felt safe: as though I had fallen asleep and were dreaming. I was a somnambulist; my body kept moving and existing in the manner that its DNA required of it. I did not even remember to pray, which was just as well; this body is not jointed in a way that permits kneeling.

Then one night, recently, I woke in the dark, my body leaning against my mate's. The side of me that didn't face her was chilled. I nuzzled her throat and she woke. I wanted her there, her moist eyes in the night. Thoughts of home had seized me in my sleep as nightmares do, and I was shaking. We grunted together for a while, then her thighs fluted and sang in that language that despite my every effort I have been unable to learn.

I just leaned into her and took solace in her nearness. "Her" I say, though the pronoun is meaningless here. I was a "him" years ago, so I call my mate "her." Isn't that strange?

My purpose here was first contact; that is what Starmind sends all the Ansibles to do. *Salaam*, we are to say. *We are here from Sol 3, and we are homo sapiens. More of us will be traveling across the void, and we want you to know us and like us.*

First contact: the idea struck me as unintelligible that night, as I leaned into her and listened to her fluting voice beneath stars whose names and numbers I didn't know. Contact, as though two disparate beings are touching for the first time. But we don't arrive here, on these other worlds, as discrete beings. We arrive as a possession, an encampment within the body of the other. The very body in which I breathe is alien to me, and despite all my psionic training and ability, my mind is in contact with neither the race of my birth nor the race among which I reside. Though I have mated and carried to term innumerable offspring and heard them squeaking in their lovely masses in the dark hollows of these salt towers, yet I am alone. No one hears me, or can.

Maybe that is why I send these thoughts out into the dark. Maybe that is why, when I wake and the world is silent and I can no longer hide within the breathing husk of this body, I still cry out sometimes, with my thoughts, or with the glossolalia of my thighbones. I cry out: Allah, Allah.

I am still, after all this wilderness of time, longing for contact.

***

I am old now. I have grown certain of it. I have been watching how these people die. They sleep standing like horses, and they die so; they go on standing until their bodies have absorbed so much salt that they become stone. They usually climb up the ridges and go out into the desert a way first; I have followed a few of them to see, though the first few times I did so, my mate tossed her head, emitting high-pitched cries that might have been panic, or fury.

But her cries did not stay me, and I have seen where the dead go.

Their statues are out there in the desert. Pilgrims who

never finished their hajj.

I will be one of them soon. This body feels slow and brittle. That is why now I climb the ridge each night and lift my whiskered face to the stars, to call out with my mind across the dark. This psicast has no real use, I fear; when I left, there was no instrument in Starmind's facility so fine-tuned as to pick up a single organism's thoughts or desires across galaxies of space and—perhaps—eons of time. But they may have more refined instruments now. And I promised the president of Starmind I would try.

I have failed every other duty.

I left two wives on earth, one who pleaded with me not to go, and one who only sorrowed in private unless she was indifferent or else secretly glad; sometimes we long for endings, even painful ones. I failed them both. I will soon abandon even the mate I have found on this planet—or one of the mates, since I cannot be sure. Nor can I know whether she will perceive this as a betrayal, or whether after the first pain of severance she will even remember me.

I only know that I vowed to report if I could. I will fail that commitment, as I have failed all others; perhaps that is why Allah has exiled me to this strange waste. Perhaps he *can* hear, he whose ear, the poet says, is pressed always to the skin of the universe. Perhaps I have simply proven unworthy of his response.

My fingers are wedged deep into the salt, and only those dry crystals against my fine hairs seem real.

This will be my last final broadcast.

ANSIBLE 15717

1

The rain reminds me of dying trees. The alibab tree of Proxima Centauri can endure only a little moisture; it is a child of the desert—though not *our* desert. The other botanists and I tried to preserve the grove that grew from the first seeds transplanted to earth, in the botanic gardens outside Kusadasi. We took such care. But in the year I turned twenty-two, a freak storm came through, lightning cutting open the sky, rain that tore holes in green leaves, stripping away fragile bark. The trees drowned in water, as children might. We strove all night to save them. I remember the bleakness before dawn, my hair slicked to my neck, my clothes drenched. I was cold and shivering. I straightened and looked out over a field of crumpled, battered things, living beings cut out of the heart of another planet, transplanted, and unable to thrive. Workers moved down the rows, slow as ghosts, searching for anything that could be saved. My face was wet not only from the downpour but from the salt of my tears. We had killed them, all these trees. I could not understand it.

***

I am a transplant, and often I have wondered if an unexpected storm will sweep in and make me die.

There are no discernible seasons here, which is strange to me. Botany is all about seasons. But here the plants just *grow*, sweating moisture in the dawn heat. I have never seen such plants on earth or any of its colonies, not even in the hydroponics bays on the moon that provide most of the food for our teeming billions. How can I possibly describe it...think of the rain forests your grandmothers told you about, the forests our planet once had but that our ancestors butchered, the ones you think are at least half mythical, where rose trees grew a hundred fifty feet high, and a thousand species of butterflies might flourish in the canopy of a single tree, waking Allah from his dreaming with their riot of hues. Think of the old vidcasts you saw in school, slow-motion capture of frogs leaping from a pool, their skin like wet paint. Back when there were frogs. Think of that. Hold those images, images of an alien world that somehow bore the same name as our own, hold those in your mind.

Then imagine a forest ten times that intense, one that could make a botanist who has harbored a secret atheism all her life suddenly kneel, head to the ground, and pray. Think of an entire ecosystem of miniature forests growing *inside* the hollow bole of a tree the size of a spaceport. Then imagine that the tree of such prodigious vitality is not even a *tree*, but only a kind of flowering weed with an exterior harder than bark, harder than granite. Imagine a single nocturnal blossom that would fill the Al-Masjid al-Haram from one wall to the other, that each night spews into the air millions of airborne spores that burn with light like violet sparks; all it would take is the feather-soft touch of just one against the back of your hand, and you would be dead before you could even gasp.

This is a world of beauty and strange poisons. An entire species of botanists could not fully catalogue it.

I remain an atheist, but now I am an atheist who prays. Allah, I am in Paradise.

***

I was twenty-three when they sent me here, yet it was no mistake or accident. I could recite the life cycle of each extraterrestrial plant by the time I was nineteen. In my twenty-first year, I published seventy-two papers on the photosynthesis of *Wolf lux*, that curious algae on the fourth moon of Wolf 359 that is so distant from its sun that its sun cannot be distinguished from a star by the naked eye. And yet it feeds and thrives. In my twenty-second year, I was appointed the first visiting fellow to the botanic gardens. *The* botanic gardens, you understand? I was what earth called an expert, and I gloried in it.

So I think Starmind must have had more than an inkling of what kind of planet this is. They were very intent on sending *me*. How they pursued me. I have never been wooed by any suitor as ardently as I was wooed by those strange, telepathic men in their absurd uniforms of black and silver. I couldn't be free of them. If I was at a restaurant, adjusting my veil slightly to tease some daring young man while pretending to be interested only in my sautéed karniyarik, sure enough, if I glanced over my shoulder I'd see two of them there, standing by a window, waiting for a polite opportunity to approach. If I took my glider on a vacation up to Ararat or to the dry, exquisitely sculpted bed of the Caspian Sea—I was making good money—I would find after a night in my tent that the Starmind recruiters had set up their own tent nearby.

They were eerie men. So silent. They must have been so used to *thinking* all the time, and listening so deeply, that they had unlearned how to make noise, how to shift their weight anxiously, how to trip over a pebble. I might be walking down an aisle in the Great Library and not even realize one was trailing me. Sometimes it scared me, a little. Mostly, I think I was flattered.

I knew what they wanted.

It certainly wasn't what I wanted. What, leave this earth, when we had just gotten it to flower again? They couldn't be serious.

It was the note I found slipped under my door one night that did it, that convinced me to take them up on this mad venture. I had been walking in the rain, and as always, this had made me sad. I kept smelling alibab leaves.

As I swung my door shut and cardlocked it, I heard the rustle as the toe of my shoe crinkled the envelope. Bending swiftly, I lifted it and snapped it open and found *paper* inside, actual *paper*. I ask you!

I unfolded it quickly. There were just thirteen words, handwritten in a bold style:

THE AMAZON WAS ALLAH'S TRINKET.
WANT TO SEE THE REAL THING?
COME QUICKLY.

So I did.

2

Every few days I walk through this forest clad in armor carved from the roots of the birdeater trees. That's what Jerome calls them, because when we first arrived we watched one catch an avian the size of a house and consume it. The word the natives use for this plant sounds like a series of rapid chirps; after much practice I can *make* the sound, but I have no idea how to *think* it or psicast it. So birdeaters it is.

These birdeaters have roots that twine through the air, with just the long, spike-shaped ends driven into the humus to drink in nutrients. The bark is very tough, and it nullifies various neurological poisons. I am grateful for this. I lost two of my team within an hour of our arrival, and two more before the first daybreak, leaving only myself and Kabul (that's Ahmad, but during training we nicknamed him after the Afghani library; if you had to listen to him for more than a minute, you'd know why), Aasfa, and Jerome (our token European).

The indigenes are as vulnerable to the poisons as we who have borrowed—*taken*—eight of their bodies. I should grieve the deaths of those eight; I am certain they *were* deaths, and I was not prepared for that. No trace of my own host remains. No one grapples with me for control of my various limbs. But when I arrived here after months of anticipation and fear, I was so relieved just to be alive. I did not grieve, nor feel guilt, and for a while I believed, wrongly, that guilt and grief were among the things I had left behind in my own body on earth, which Starmind had warned me would be incinerated by the force of my transfer here.

The indigenes who found us after that transfer were kind to us; they did not understand the damage that had befallen these eight members of their tribe, and they cared for us, as we would for invalids back in Cairo. They were the ones who taught us about the birdeater roots.

We wear the armor of roots whenever we must climb to find the sun, to convert its light to sugar, to energy; once every few days, we rise to the canopy and feast. We sleep during the night within the pitcher-shaped leaves of the milk-maker plant, leaves that cup us like a mother's hands, closing around us, translucent like a seashell, walling out the night's spores and nocturnal predations. There is room in each for two or at most three. I sleep with Aasfa, who I have found to be a gentle lover. She has soft skin and fierce eyes, and I always liked her, even during training, though we never touched or did anything intimate until after our arrival here. Kabul is promiscuous and sleeps with whatever native will have him. Jerome sleeps alone, and wakes at dawn with a haggard face. He tried to lecture me once and I laughed at him. I'd heard the Europeans had backwards notions but I had met so few of them in my work that I hadn't given thought to it before.

At first I couldn't believe Jerome was serious. "We're not even *human*," I told him, waving six of my hands before his face.

"We're human in our hearts." He was gruff, but I could see that his eyes had tinted green with fear.

"Well, not the same kind of human," I told him. "And even if we were, what does any of that matter here?"

That made him angry, and that triggered a hormonal response in both of our bodies, so that we attacked and tore at each other for a few hours. His mind had transferred into a stronger body than my own, and I had the worst of it; he left me scarred, with great gashes along my flanks. I crawled back to our local profusion of milk-maker plants, mewing with pain, fury chemicals still igniting and roaring through my body. He returned before I did, and I found him standing in the midst of a dozen of the natives. His six long hands beat at his narrow, stalklike belly, as though he were a gorilla. His chirping and squeaking was high and piercing, and easily the loudest thing in the forest. He was trying to impress his views on our host species. The body he inhabited had been previously tenanted by one of the voices of the people, one who was esteemed and respected. So they were listening to him, though the leaves on their backs were drying, yellowing with confusion.

It is a failing of mine that I have never been patient with people. Plants live vivaciously, even if they live too slowly for most people on earth to care. Plants do what needs to be done, and they don't quibble over it or doubt themselves: they just do. They just *live*. And they are the original inhabitants of our world, the pioneers, the founders of our inheritance. They make the very air we breathe. For centuries, they provided the pages on which we wrote everything that we are. To this day, the sacred Quran itself is inscribed on plant matter.

Where better should we learn how to live?

I have no patience for people. Fury surged into me like dark sap, impossible to contain. I crept up behind Jerome. His listeners, still confused, gave no sign to warn him. I took his third spine in my hands, all my long fingers curled around it, strong as cedar branches, and I snapped him.

3

Jerome still has the use of his conscious mind, and his secondary brain controlling memory and language. But his third brain, the one that controls glands for producing chemicals that trigger aggression responses—that one is disabled, cut off from the rest of his body. He can *think* aggressively, perhaps, but he cannot *feel* aggressive. He is helpless; some evenings, he has to be carried to his vegetable bed.

I have had time to regret the violence I did, which is a violence that belongs to this new body, a violence that I don't understand. I try not to think about it much.

He has taken to singing, some nights. His chirpings and warblings tug at the heart. Sometimes they lullaby us to sleep; sometimes they leave us mewing in sorrow all night. I remember one night when, after our love, Aasfa and I twined our bodies tightly together, becoming nearly a single stalk, and mewed the same note together, unceasing, for hours. Jerome has that power over all of us, both native and earthborn.

I don't know what he is mourning, exactly: how much of it is the injury I did him, or how much is a yearning for his small house in Belarus. I think he is trying to recreate, in his singing, the worship songs of his own religion and his own people. Most of it is gibberish, untranslatable into this planet's language, but though we don't have his ideas or his words, he makes us feel what he feels, for a time.

Aasfa tried to put it into words once as she caressed me gently. "When I was sixteen, I thought she was immortal. Then one day—an aneurism, and my mother was gone before I could even tell her how I loved her, before I could wish her well. Just gone, like a light switched off, as simply and quickly as that. I think of her, when Jerome sings. That sadness that carves a hole into the heart and curls up inside it for a while: Jerome's music makes me feel that again."

"He makes me think it is raining," I answered, my body moving under her touch. "He makes me remember dying trees."

***

An alibab tree grows from a round bulb that you can hold in the palm of your hand. Once the sprout has broken free, the bulb seals itself and begins to absorb water. Eventually it will expand to the size of a woman's head, and will hold all the water the tree needs to sustain itself for years at a time.

When I was twenty-two, I once spent an entire evening perched in the intricate branches of an alibab, holding a dormant bulb in my hand. It was furred on the outside, like a coconut, and that soft skin of the plant felt gentle on my palm. I am sure I took as much pleasure in it as any woman in Cairo has ever taken in a cat, or any woman in Athens in a parakeet. The Europeans who first discovered the alibab—the first living thing they encountered on another planet—had named this organism whimsically after a character from old stories who could unlock hidden treasuries. Gazing at the locked treasury of this small bulb, I realized I had become bored with writing papers, and that the actual work of transplanting the alibab grove was done. I felt that evening that if I could only see into the hollow space within that bulb, or sense something more than mere tactile sensation through my hands (which were now calloused from fieldwork), maybe I would not be bored but enlightened. Remember, I was an atheist then. (I am not sure what I am now. Because I have only a few hours left, at most, I will probably never find out.)

That bulb—the way it felt in my hand—and the complete *secret*ness of it, is one of the things I remember most from my time at the botanical gardens outside Kusadasi. One of the others is a kiss from a man beneath that same alibab; he wore the same uniform green I did, and his eyes were green also, but not the green that we wore. His irises were the alien hue of the alibab leaves; they fascinated me. His kiss did, too. I don't remember how it felt; I no longer have lips to feel it. But I remember how much I enjoyed it. Our liaison was brief and heated and fated to end quickly; I didn't want entanglements, and he was a local, and Shiite. It would not have worked.

And yet, I remember his hands as he draped absorbent cloths over the trees, when the rain fell so hard it was difficult to breathe in it. I remember the fury in his eyes as he tore at the sodden earth with a shovel, other workers beside him, digging trenches and lining them with foil to catch and hold the water, to keep the runoff from the next garden from swamping our fragile alibabs. I remember weeping as I struggled with a humidity controller that had sputtered out, and I recall his hand against mine, unexpectedly lending his strength on the wrench. I remember the roar as the machine came to life, blasting hot, dry air out over our work. Our gazes met, and, for a moment, I nearly loved him.

***

Allah may be a fiction of men's dreams, or a deity infinite and all-compassionate, or he may be the photosynthetic system that translates some unknown light into the energies that blaze at the heart of our universe. Whether the Quran is his inerrant word or only scribbles on the pulp of a dead plant, I pray, thanking him that we did not save the alibabs, that I did not risk becoming a wife. That I did not stay on earth. That I have seen all I have seen. Even suffering as I do now, I would not have given up one moment of this strange life in this strange body, not even for another kiss from that attractive Shiite in Kusadasi.

***

The lift from Kusadasi to Cairo took only three hours but felt much longer. I didn't look out at the clouds, or at the sea passing below. The whole way, I focused on the bulb I held between my palms, in my lap: the dormant alibab, its fur soft against my fingers but damp, as though I were consoling a bedraggled kitten. Everything else in the grove had been dead by morning; there was only this, like a seed or an unhatched egg. I don't know why I took it with me, as though somewhere on earth I might find a place where it belonged. As though there might be such a place. The other passengers in my compartment, a Jewish rabbi with a Torah disk pendant around his neck and a veiled, elderly woman in purple robes with a bioengineer's mark by her left eye, eyed me curiously, but I ignored them. I was completely preoccupied with the unsettling thought that the lift would take me home to Cairo, but that the alibab and I both would be strangers there.

When we transplant a tree—or a person—or an idea to a new climate, we are taking a great risk. We do not know if it will drown, like an alibab in our rains, or thrive and perhaps overtake and overwhelm, like the rabbits did in Australia or like Christianity in the Americas. A stray pollen might rewrite an ecosystem. A transplant is an inherently violent thing, an infection of a local climate by a new and random element. It is unpredictable. Anything can happen.

4

Aasfa was the only one who noticed my restlessness, and she spoke with me about it two nights ago.

"What is it?" she asked me as I stirred, as I had for hours. "What's bothering you?"

I didn't have much of an answer. As closely as I could guess, we had been here several months, but the unease was new; I'd first felt it a few nights before. It was getting worse. It was like a scraping against the edge of my mind, or like rat's feet scratching inside a wall. It wasn't a sound; it wasn't even a sense of being observed. Just the sense of something vile and pestilent and much too near. Just out of hearing, just out of sight. Some nights, the feeling had been so acute that I lay trembling, hardly daring to speak or move for fear that the invisible, scraping *thing* would be stirred and summoned out of the dark. I wondered if this was what tall stalks of rhubarb feel when scurrying rodents brush by, barely sensible from the perspective of a plant whose leaves know only how to touch the air and sun, and whose roots know only how to touch earth and water— barely sensible, yet menacing, the approach of a predator that can be neither fled nor reasoned with nor even truly detected until the first gnawing, until its teeth chop deeply into the plant's body.

***

"I don't know," I told Aasfa. "Bad dreams."

She moved gently against me, in the dark.

Tell me your dreams, she psicast at me, forming words in Arabic in my mind, as we had been trained to do. *Everything is good for us now, and we are fat with sunlight. What troubles you?*

But I didn't answer. I liked the sharing of our bodies, but felt uncomfortable psicasting with her. Sometimes the mind is too intimate a thing to share.

I waited until Aasfa was asleep and her three stalks were clacking quietly, rhythmically against each other in the dreamsleep of our tribe on this world. Then I crept from our bed in the milk-maker leaves, careful not to disturb the botanical samples and cuttings I'd collected in orderly rows on the ground below our bed. I drew on my armor of birdeater bark, soothed by the clicking of our sleeping people, all around me. Except from Jerome's bed, which, for once, was silent. The canopy life hooted and howled far above me, in high boughs nearer the stars, but I didn't worry about these noises in the dark. They were not a threat.

Yet there *was* a threat.

I was sure of it.

This alien body, *my* body, was rushing with fear-chemicals. I was still human enough, still animal enough, to go look for the threat, rather than plant myself deep and wait.

I strode into the deep forest. I did not get lost. On this world, we have more senses and we are fiercely aware of every change about us. We know how saturated the humus beneath our feet is with water, we know the humidity, the air pressure. We can sense the passage of air as a hookfly flits toward us, or the deep pool of damp air that fills a trapper-hunter's pit before our feet. We are tightly attuned and fragile, though something in us burns hot as the heart of a swamp. In little time I found myself standing where my colleagues and I had first arrived on this planet. It was not far from our colony of milk-maker plants, because the eight bodies our minds seized and inhabited when we arrived had been on their journey up from the milk-maker colony to meet the sun.

I looked carefully around me, peering between the stalks of mighty plants. Something was here. Somewhere. I began exploring the site in slow circles, each larger than the last. I don't know how much time passed as I searched. A lot, I think. I explored mostly by scent, not sight; the nights are dark this far under the canopy. But by luck, I caught a faint luminescence—and a hint of ammonia— some distance away. Moving toward it, I nearly slid; the humus here was infected with a vile slime, like the stories mollusks leave behind them on earth. I reacted to it much as my former body might have to a slug. But I followed it.

The luminescent thing was a flaccid, empty skin, like some boneless organism vomited up on the shore—or like the body of an animal emptied of its insides by maggots. It was corpse-white and it glowed faintly. It was immense, as though I stood near a collapsed pavilion. At first I thought it dead—if it had been alive at all—but a few of its cilia moved slightly. I bent over it like a tree in the wind, peering at those tender filaments. Fear crashed through me in waves of violent chemicals. The thing beneath me had no sight organs that I could detect; yet it seemed to *see* me. It seemed as though the thing *was* an eye. And a mouth. And a malevolent, creeping mind.

It did not belong here.

Not in this place of hot, teeming life.

***

I fled, emitting high-pitched sounds as I did. I didn't want to know what I had found at our arrival site, I didn't want to study it or classify it or stay anywhere at all near it. It was nothing botanical, nothing truly animal either, and only the thought that it seemed to be dying and could not follow me kept me from tumbling into a chemical bath of madness.

Other thoughts shot through me as I ran. That where there was one such thing, there might be others. That I, a scientist, should be ashamed of my flight. That if I stopped for even a few seconds, something would catch me—not that wounded thing behind me, surely, but something for which it was only a pale mannequin. That if one Ansible team could arrive here from our world, perhaps other things could arrive here from other worlds.

By the time I returned, I was shaking, flakes of my vegetable skin sloughing from me to the ground; I was ill, I was falling apart. These bodies are not made for such a rapid pace, and only bolt after bolt of chemicals had kept me running. I fell into the leaves of our plant desperate for sunlight and sugar and food, my mind still fracturing into a million fears inside me. And there I found Aasfa twitching in her sleep.

***

Or not in her sleep.

Her many eyes were all opened, opened *wide* as though they had been peeled open, forced open, until they were in danger of losing their moisture and drying like hard, cracked pebbles. Her mouths—long, slitlike orifices meant not for kissing or for speech but for collecting rainwater and for inhaling carbon dioxide—were open, too. One was slack; the other let out a dry rasp of air on each exhale, an almost-sound, like screaming from a throat that is so hoarse it can no longer release any sound but that of escaping air.

I went cold with horror. Wrapping my hands about her second stalk, I shook her, and again. She didn't appear to notice me. What was happening to her? I cried out, several times, and others came, opening up our milk-maker bed and peering in, their leaves pale with worry. All but Jerome, who began to sing mournfully from his own milk-maker plant.

"What is it?" Kabul demanded. One of his lovers

peered, blinking, through the gap between his stalks.

"It's Aasfa! Something is wrong. Something is so wrong."

Gently, we pulled her out of the milk-maker plant and lay her on the humus below. We gathered around her, chirping and checking her stalks with our hands, searching for some fracture or break. But there was nothing. No reason for her to be like this. Panic spread, moist and cold, through my body, and I struck Kabul, hard, and he rolled aside across the ground and came up with his eyes blazing, and I knew that in another moment we would all be attacking each other, driven by chemicals that are stronger than conscious thought, all triggered by the fear pheromones I was pumping into the air around me.

Then one of the others—not one of our Ansible team—chirped at us, high and piercing, and, shuddering as we fought for control of our bodies, we turned and saw what he had found. I stared with all my eyes. A pale tendril or a thread, so fine it could only be seen when it caught the dim light, was wrapped about Aasfa's second stalk, like a child's string on earth. It was tight, and had bitten into her skin, so that even as I watched, her stalk turned a dark, rotted green around it. I grabbed for the tendril, seized it, meaning to snap it, but it was strong as wire. Aasfa twitched violently as I pulled at it, and I stumbled away from her, shrilling my dismay.

"The thread disappears into the dark, over there." Kabul pointed. He was right. It vanished into the shadows under the trees. Something out there, somewhere, was tethered to her. In another instant, I realized that the thread disappeared in the direction of our arrival site. It glinted and flashed in and out of visibility, as Aasfa spasmed and jerked; its pale, fleshy color was the same as that of the dying invertebrate I had encountered less than an hour before.

***

When my panic abated, several of us were dead and another was broken and dying; the rest of us stood quivering like leaves brushed by some forest behemoth. I trembled with the force of the chemicals that were still surging and rushing through all the cell structures of my body. Kabul was still on his feet too, and also the one who had found the thread. Aasfa lay very still, but her mouths were making that terrible exhalation, and I knew she was alive.

Jerome was singing.

His song had quieted the panic, the instinctive fear and fury that had seized first me, then others. His song was sad and old and made me think of earth; my eyes moistened— one of the few facts of biology that this body shares with my original one. I stared down at Aasfa. I didn't know how long our people had assailed each other, how long we'd shrieked and torn. I only knew that as long as we had, Aasfa had been suffering. My gaze followed that tendril, that violent wire, into the forest, and a moment later, I was loping after it. Kabul cried out behind me; I did not stop, and soon I heard the others following.

I let Jerome's song get inside me while I ran, let it

soothe the violence in my body. The odor of ammonia grew; I glanced all about for evidence of that trail of slime, but saw nothing. The foliage grew thicker, and I was very aware that the others were following me without armor, without protection if we should run through a burst of toxic spores or encounter a poisonous amphibian. But I did not slow; I could think only of Aasfa.

Kabul is larger than I, and was less fatigued; he overtook me and ran ahead, psicasting back, telling me to be calm, to stop and think, that whatever predator lay ahead was something unknown, both to us and to our adopted species, that we needed to be cautious and *human*. I was not human that night, and I didn't answer him.

The dark was lightening as this world swung toward the sun, and in the dimness ahead, perhaps halfway to our arrival site, I saw Kabul edge carefully around a trapper-hunter's wide pit, avoiding the insect's lair; I followed. Then Kabul stopped suddenly near the bole of a vast bird-eater tree, larger than most. I dug into the earth and stopped also. He was twitching, his limbs jerking as though in a seizure. With my mind, I called out his name, but there was no answer. One of his stalks began tapping rhythmically against another, as though he were asleep and dreaming. Suddenly, something unseen pulled him into the air; he hung out of reach. There was a new sound above me; I strained to hear it: a rasping exhalation. I trembled with dread. It was the same sound, the *same* silent scream I'd heard from Aasfa.

There were chirping cries behind me. Then the others were darting past me to stand just below Kabul's borrowed and dangling body. Seized by premonition, I cried a warning. Even as I did, several of my companions began jerking and shuddering, their voices silenced, and then they were wrenched into the air. Then a few more, and the others fell back, shrieking and clicking in terror.

Glancing up, I saw hundreds, perhaps thousands of tendrils drifting slowly down through the dim air like threads of Turkish silk. One curled about a young female's stalk and she twitched as though stung with poison. I screamed another warning, then ducked low. But before I did, I saw it, I *saw* it, just a *glimpse* of it, just enough that I want to scream now, remembering it: something immense and pale, glistening like a jellyfish just lifted from the sea. It had fastened itself to the bark of the tree and grown into it like some loathsome fungus. I only saw it for an instant, then it was as though I were looking into a shadow in my peripheral vision. A blur, nothing more. It had concealed itself.

I danced like a dandelion stalk in the wind, striving to avoid the wispy tendrils. All around me, tendrils caught the others, lifting them and holding them in moments of terror, transfixed and jerking in the air like fish in the anemone's grip. Helpless.

But I am from earth.

I still remember life in a body that had more movement, *different* movement. I think that is what saved me, me only out of all our people, and only barely.

I threw myself about, dodging and spinning before those long wisps of silk could touch me.

In another heartbeat, I saw myself all but surrounded by threads, as though I peered at the world through a curtain; desperate, I ducked back, then threw myself into a leap across the trapper-hunter's pit behind me, a leap that only a human body could have managed. Yet I knew as I leaped that I could make it. I could escape. Then a tendril caught my third stalk in a cold grip like wire.

***

For a terrible eternity, I was somewhere else. Somewhen else. There was thunder louder than I had ever heard it; I was running barefoot, in a human body, in *my* human body, through mud, through a sliding avalanche of wet earth. The world had tipped. Alibab trees were toppling with wooden groans and then sliding down wildly through the mud, and I had to dodge them or leap over them, screaming for them not to die, though I could see them bloating with water, each of them sickly and near bursting, their bark sloughing away. I caught one in my hands and tried to stop it, but rolled down with it. Tried to keep the bark from sliding off the tree as we rolled, but it crumbled like wet bread beneath my fingers. And then we tumbled together, the tree and I, over a precipice and there was a roar of mud falling over us and with us, and far below us in the dark a terrible unseen presence that reached for me with a thousand tiny, slender fingers. Something that would eat me. Something that would eat every tree that had ever grown. Something that would eat the universe. Shrieking, I fell toward it.

***

Then the world broke and shattered like glass; there was light all around me, then an impact that left me stunned. I lay still, senseless though awake. After a time I realized that I was lying at the pit's bottom. The moss of the pit was dry under my back, so I knew it was long disused, the trapper insect that lived here long dead; yet I was trapped, all the same. Far above me were swaying—and *still* sway—the twitching bodies of the people of this planet, like so many gutted fish or broken marionettes, each lost in a nightmare of their own, their minds ingested slowly while they dream. I know this because when I reach toward them with my mind, I feel theirs flickering and faint, siphoning away. Every one of them—all of these beautiful people who climb trees vast as continents to drink the sun—every one of them is being eaten from within. A few tendrils drift above me without a victim as though stirred by a wind I cannot feel. But none of them reach for me. None of them know I am here.

5

I am broken as Jerome was broken. My third stalk is snapped, cracked in the tension between my leap, the tendril that seized me, and gravity. I lie here thinking that I should rise and find some way to flee, but without any will to. I have energy only for psicasting, and for singing. I make music as Jerome made music, I make music as I heard dervishes make music in the great Sufi dance halls of Basra and Baghdad and Istanbul, when I was a girl. I loved them with a fierce and passionate love, the way other young girls loved puppies or their favorite toys, because the dervishes were beautiful to me: they spun and leapt and spun again like leaves in a tempest, like dandelion seeds in the summer air. They were not human, these dancing fools, these wise poets: they were plants. Moving as plants move, only faster. Rejoicing in life as plants do, only louder. Leaping as plants leap, from the earth toward the sun, unable ever to reach it yet driven drunkenly, madly to try. How I loved them!

Now I sing as they did.

***

The dying sway above me. Sometimes I hear one or two of them clicking. They are dreaming. They are all dreaming. Recalling my own nightmare when the tendril touched me, I fear for them. Time is not the same when we sleep. Not even for plants. How many nightmares have they each endured—Kabul, and my lovely Aasfa, and all the others—in the time that I have lain here dying in this pit?

I have had time to think.

The creature, the *thing*, arrived where we did, and left its wounded companion behind—unless there is only one, and by feeding on Aasfa it revived itself. Though I am not devout, I hardly believe in coincidences. Whatever that thing is, that demon of terror and hunger, whether polyp or fungus or jinn with no proper place or phylum in Allah's vegetable creation, whatever it is, there can be only one reason why its point of arrival was identical to our own. It *followed* us across the seedless and desert void.

It came here from earth.

6

It is raining.

I hear Jerome singing in the distance. How can anyone that lonely sound so beautiful? Maybe he is the only one of us left, besides me, the only one uncaught. And we are both maimed and alone. My heart is thick with regret as I join my voice to his.

It is raining on my face, and I cannot tell the tears from the water. Trees, an entire people of trees, are dying, up there. Only a few still move; most hang brittle like dried-up cones after a summer blaze. But this world is not dry, it is never dry; I lie in the mud. Water pours in a rush over the sides of the pit. But I am a plant; what have I to fear from falling water? It is so beautiful, streaming down at me, like silver hair; I will lie here singing to it, until I die.

ANSIBLE 2

We are a people of both song and science. Each morning after muezzin I rise from my knees, roll up my prayer rug, and descend into paradise beneath the Starmind facility. The descent itself is routine—retinal scans and DNA checks and a long drop chute that I enjoyed when I was younger but now the rush of it makes me fall asleep. And always at the bottom the same airlock, unchanged, silent, a work of dark and opaque glass too thick to break. If my dreams the night before have been particularly harrowing, I crouch and peer at the glass, looking for small scratches, such as those that might be left in panic by fingernails. But no, the glass is always clear. Small drops of condensation on the other side, like minute creatures clinging to the skin of the world. A sigh from me and a sigh from the airlock, and I am through.

The interior is a profusion of greenery sweating moisture and swelling in on the narrow, irregular paths of hard stone. The paradise is a labyrinth, if you like, but I need no Greek golden thread to find my way through it or back out; it is mine. I designed it. It contains at its heart the most monstrous things I have ever seen or regretted, and like the architect I am locked in with them, so that the horrors are always about me, even when seventy floors of science and technology and intense training and laboratories separate me from this place. They are closest at night. I wake shivering in my bed in the dark and imagine that I can hear them, broken from their silver coffins, their fingers scratching at the glass, scratching, always scratching.

I take hard stimulants in the morning. I have to.

I don't sleep well.

Or at all, some nights.

***

The Arabs in this nation tell legends of the Old Man of the Mountain, whom Salah ah Din destroyed but who ruled the desert with cunning and cruelty, backed not by any army of camel archers but by a brotherhood of assassins addicted to the Old Man's drugs and granted visions of paradise before their death. Vast gardens laid out to his design with naked girls set loose like deer to run between the trees or bathe in the rock pools, to be hunted and caught and enjoyed. *Such a place will be yours*, the Old Man would whisper into the hazed minds of his acolytes, *if you are faithful.*

What drug makes *my* brain shimmer with mirages?

What do I believe I will gain and enjoy, in this garden?

Why do I, amid so many horrors, remain faithful?

***

Enough. That is an Arab fantasy, not mine. I am a sane man, of the Muslim East. I studied in the University Underwater, in sunken Jakarta. My mentors were the finest psychologists, linguists, and psionicists in the world. I learned from them that our minds weave stories like vast and colorful tapestries out of the many threads of our experiences and others', but those tapestries are only artworks, they are not real.

No stories, whether West, Middle, or East, can prepare me for the dark heart of this paradise. I approach it now, and the wet fronds of surrounding foliage against my skin are a strange, cooling comfort, the only comfort left to me: a reminder that even if the world withers we might regrow it, we *are* regrowing it. Just a little, a very little at a time. We walk hand in hand out of the desert and the violence of our past, violence against our brother and violence against the earth itself, and we will see this world become forest if it takes us a thousand generations. And then at last we will be ready for the stars. My work will be redeemed and the road will have been mapped for our travels, a million emissaries gone before us to greet those who keep their oases in that vaster Sahara in which every dung fire is a blazing sun and the bedouins who gather about it have no human faces.

***

In the midst of the garden, the cryotubes are held in a suspension net that glistens like the webs spiders make, and it extends all the way to the ceiling and thirty meters to my left and thirty to my right, with the lowest of the cryotubes level with my knees and the highest far above my head, and just enough space between each for a man to lie down on one without being crushed by the one above it. If any man could bear to lie there.

I bend at the knees and peer inside one of the low tubes. It is bioglass, of course, and the inside is frosted but you can see through in patches of lucid clarity. Through one, I can see the face of the sleeping corpse: a frozen youth with dark skin. Ansible 15703, I think. Second member of his team. An anthropologist from the Remnant of the Congo. I reach for his name, but can't recall it. His mouth is frosted, and his eyelids, and he looks as though he is floating in air, though I know the tube is filled with liquid and vacuum-sealed. He has been in there four months, and he may be in there four years or forty or forever, if we do not learn some way to save him.

Mercifully, his eyes are closed; most of the others aren't. We have frozen them, but brain activity remains, minimal yet alarming: high levels of norepinepherine and dopamine, an amygdala that refuses to be quiescent though the heart rate has slowed to one beat per month. He can't be *conscious* as we understand *consciousness*, yet, on a purely animal level, his body might be experiencing terror, anguish, and ongoing panic though slowed to the life pulse of a planet.

I straighten and let my gaze flick over the other tubes. So many have their eyes open, unseeing yet frozen in a moment of fear. What *did* they experience, my Ansibles, at the instant of transfer into an alien body on an alien world? The link should have remained open: if it had worked, they should have been able to report, to speak with us through their bodies here on earth. But instead...the screams. Men and women I had loved and trained, convulsing and jerking on the floor. How many teams I have flung into the dark, each time with a new adjustments on instruments that *should* work, instruments that have helped us establish stable ansible connections in mice and in macaws and in small infants but not in any human old enough to speak. But we are almost there, we are going to do it. And maybe these minds *did* arrive at their destinations, maybe even now they inhabit and manipulate bodies on their target worlds, and the pure animal panic exists only in these, their ruins here in my facility. No way to know.

All those eyes staring at me.

Almost I can hear their fingernails scratching the edges of my mind, as I heard them in my sleep scratching at their capsules, scratching at the door. Almost I can imagine them crying out to me, silently, psi screams to go with the physical ones I remember hearing. But it is only my imagination, only my guilt.

The cryotubes holding Ansible 1 are on the far side of this shining net. I make my way to them, whispering the words of the first sura under my breath, a recitation that calmed me when I was younger. I trail my fingers along the sleek surface of one of the capsules, feeling the bioglass ripple around my skin, sucking very gently at the epidermis but doing little to slow my hand. Though the inside of the glass looks like winter, the outside that touches my skin is warm, a reminder that insides and outsides rarely correspond. But the capsules feel *real* and that is the assurance I need: that I walk waking in my facility and am not treading the darker garden of my dreams again. Being awake is one of my only comforts.

I had others, once. After the second prayer I used to take fifteen minutes to watch aerial vids of the Broken Shore and the stunted forests of my youth. In the hour after dawn, I would relinquish all stresses and remember myself in the soft clasp of Ahava's body around me. And in the evenings I used to take great delight in brewing coffee imported from the hydroponics bays on the moon. Most people are stimulated by coffee; I find that it helps me sleep, particularly with warm milk. The scent of it soothes me, as does its rich, dark color. I used to tap my spoon three times against the cup I poured, a little ritual. Now I no longer do so; I have hired someone to brew coffee for me, and when I hear tapping against a ceramic surface, it makes my palms sweat.

I watched Ansible 1 depart from a console in my quarters, and I brewed coffee to calm my nerves. The cameras were implanted in the leaves of a pomegranate tree in the garden atrium on the sixty-second floor of the facility. That gave me a view from above as the four men and two women of team Ansible 1 meditated, then finished their evening prayer; then, just as I poured my cup, they established the link with foreign bodies in some far other place. I tapped my cup three times, staring at the images, and that was how long it took before the first screams.

***

We ran tests on the six bodies of Ansible 1. Oh, we ran tests. Night after night, working triple shifts in the best laboratories my funds could purchase. We had to understand what had happened. It has been six years, and we are no closer. All these bodies stare at me as I meet their gaze, one after the other, shying away from none. And I can hear none of their screams. Only the soft noise the cryotubes themselves make, like the sound of one leaf rubbing gently against another.

None of the teams can know of this place. Only I come here. I have told the new trainees that the energy expenditure of establishing an ansible incinerates the original body but leaves the mind intact within the distant host. That last part may even be true, is likely true. I hope it is. So much I haven't told them. That the connection can only be made across time, so that they are transferring not only into distant space but into distant future. We have told some of the teams what kind of bodies to expect, what kind of climate, whether they will appear on a planet or an asteroid or some far artifact. Other teams, we've told nothing. Musa, the neuropsichemist I borrowed from First Psionic Medical, suggested that secrecy, with his nasal voice and his watery eyes that unnerve me when I look at them too long. Chemicals in the brain, he tells me – everything has its origin in chemicals in the brain. Maybe the excitement of curiosity or the fright at the unknown might prove the crucial ingredient to permit a successful transfer, or the calm of knowledge, or the steadiness of faith. All of these are chemical reactions lit like little fires in the mine by torches held by ourselves or by Allah. Who can say which will burn a path free to a new world?

I am now convinced Musa is half mad himself.

But that does not make him wrong.

***

Last, I stand by Ahava's cylinder. She was a Jew, and her name always sounded strange on my tongue, but her name was right for her. I still remember the scent of her hair when I held her. Today her face is still young, as mine is not. I touch the glass above her mouth and watch the ripples shimmer across her unveiled features. My throat tightens, but I do not cry; I used up all my tears long ago. I just call to her a few times with my mind, as I do each morning, no longer hoping vainly for a reply, but because I have done this ritual so many times it would be unthinkable not to. It is written into my days as surely as my DNA is written into my body. *Ahava,* I whisper into the dark, *Ahava.* She had more psionic training than I, but I can usually touch another's mind, feel it stir beneath my touch even as the bioglass does beneath my palm as I press it now over her cheek. But her mind—and the few others here I have risked calling out to—has become strange. Rather than swimming through fluid toward the living presence of another, reaching for her is like tumbling through a vast empty place alive with whispers. I have to pull myself free with a gasp, but I have become practiced at it. I never tumble in completely.

Maybe she *is* empty, and only those whispers are left of her. Or maybe she's empty like a room that she has left, and she lives on now four hundred and seventeen years in the future, one hundred and sixty light years away, in a body fastened like a lamprey to an immense, sentient biomass adrift in the atmosphere of a gas giant her team was to visit. Maybe she persists within the flesh of that symbiote. But I will never again touch her or hear her voice. Her face is still beneath my hand, beneath the living glass.

She was the second to step into the dark. Ansible 2, before we began numbering the Ansibles in the tens of thousands to convince ourselves that we were more practiced at this than we are. I argued with her bitterly the night before she went. I even struck her, and to this day I carry the shame of it. She went pale as a European and then her eyes were dark and hot with wrath and she left my quarters without speaking another word. Nor did she speak to me before transferring out, and I knew she had gone only because of the screams of the medics who found her body twitching and kicking in the lab. Cold panic took me and I ran through the facility—a blur of white walls and white doors and my body suddenly strange to me, no longer really under my control, my skin numb as if it received no input regarding the heat or dryness of the air—until I skidded to a stop by the overturned table, crashing to my knees amid the scatter of sterile instruments and samples, to take her and lift her in my arms, crushing her to me, the weight of her body against my breast the only thing preventing my sobs from breaking me apart, breaking me like the glass vials now shattered on the floor, all that I was spilled out across my own facility.

***

I waited too long to freeze her. I was desperate, hopeful that I could find some way to recover her mind, pull her back fully into her body. Nothing worked. Strapped to a medic's stretcher, her mouth open, screaming silently and without sound for hours and hours and hours, and finally I screamed too, less silently. Taking up one of the long metal psi concentration sensors, I chased the medics from the lab and then I smashed all of it, everything, the readers, the translators, the psionic interference dampers, every interface and every cold, sleek surface of machinery in that place. Until I stood in a cloud of tiny fragments and motes of metal dust, no longer screaming but panting, my body slick with sweat, my hands cramped about the sensor rod. All of this beautiful technology and none of it had kept my Ahava safe. None of it had brought her or any of us one day nearer the stars. I was on my knees again, not sure how that had happened, just weeping and whimpering that one word over and over again, the word I'd been screaming, whether I'd meant it as plea or prayer or cry of rage. "*Allah ... Allah ... Allah...*"

***

Now she is frozen, frozen for all time. Her eyes are open, her mouth too. But there is no life in them, just frost on her lashes and her lips. I rest my hands on the cold glass and peer in at her, my breathing troubled. I want to tell myself lies. I want to tell myself that she is this day in paradise, one greater by far than this artificial one in which I have lain her capsule. I want to tell myself that her spirit is at peace in the infinite compassion of Allah that fills the universe the way light fills a room, exerting little pressure on what it touches yet making the otherwise dark room livable and a joy. I want to tell myself that if I were to walk out into the badlands and listen to the wind, I would hear her laughter, out there in the empty places with Allah. She is what others would call an infidel, I suppose, but she and I, we never believed that. There are times when the thought of her unbelief would leave me anxious, but her own faith was written so deeply on her heart that I could only believe the fingers of Allah himself had inscribed it there.

So I yearn to tell myself that she has found *islam* and *salaam*, though her body has not. Yet I know this is a lie. I saw the scans of her brain. I know that in founding this Starmind Project, in speaking with her in whispers after our love in the quiet time before dawn, sharing with her my desire for the stars, my longing to touch with my own mind the thoughts of those who were born drinking in the energy of an alien sun, in loving her, in opening my heart to her, I doomed her. Better for her to have married another infidel Jew, as her mother wished. The *kebaya* she wore when I kissed her at our wedding was for her the gown of a psionic trauma patient, though neither of us knew it.

"But *why* don't you want me to go?" Ahava had cried, that final night.

"I just *don't*." Which was no answer. But I couldn't tell her, couldn't tell her about Ansible 1, couldn't risk it; she would insist on telling the others, and that was the one thing that could never happen, not ever. The one thing that would bring in the ayatollah to close the doors on Starmind and on humanity's future. And this project of ours has never been for the ayatollah and his imams, this project is something Allah lit like a blaze in my heart and I only will burn in its flame, until the last embers of my burning light humanity's way across the last desert.

"Tell me," she cried, her eyes on fire. I had never seen her so beautiful. "Tell me. If you have ever loved me at all, *tell me*. You have lain inside me; now let me inside that heart you hold so close. What have you done, Takwan? Tell me what you have done!"

***

The climb back up into the facility from the garden I've made for her is slow and silent. Though I am late, I take the time to make the ascent properly. I visit paradise to remember its cost; that keeps me human and Muslim, submitted to the will of Allah. Now I close my eyes; my feet remember the upward journey well enough. Before the eyes of my mind I summon, one after the other, my memories of the badlands and the dead seas and the devastated world around us: a world dessicated by those who came before us. I remember the places I have seen, the sites I visited as a young man with Ahava, before I dared to dream of the Starmind project. The dirty ice of the Arctic, the little of it that is left. The Amazon desert, poisonous now and a graveyard of emptied cities. The sunken trash fields covering the Atlantic sea bed in meters-deep plastic and metal.

The past is the desert. The present is our hajj across the waste. The future is the paradise we yearn for, moist and fecund, where the corpses of our violent acts are entombed in no cryotubes but instead returned to the silt and soil and converted into living matter again in a greenery greater than what we have lost.

***

Avoiding the labs this morning, I visit the trainee teams one at a time. Some are in the sensory deprivation rooms preparing themselves for the void, others are exercising their bodies, as devotedly as athletes would. The 15716 team is in the briefing library, studying my carefully scripted lies. I visit the 15715 team last, Malala's team, because hers will depart today. They are ready.

They are my secret. My prayer and my defiant shout

into the void.

Arriving, I wait a few moments at the door. The team members are each speaking into small, steel missives, recording their farewells to loved ones. I watch their lips moving, their cheeks wet with tears or their eyes glistening with tears held back. I smooth the wrinkles in my uniform of black and silver; when I stand before the Ansibles, I have to look—and be—perfect. I must project confidence and peace and a formidable will. How can I ask them to accept the lies I give them, if anything about me looks careless or tentative?

Hasna is the first to look up. She gives a start when she sees me, and averting her eyes quickly, she whispers a word to the woman to her left. That woman is Malala Ali, and she rises at once gracefully to her feet.

She is Iranian, dark-eyed, and lovely. I try not to think about that, though it has been a long time since I held Ahava in my arms. I can't think about any of these young women and men that way. I am sending them into nightmares. They are already bodies behind frosted glass, nothing more.

She lowers her eyes respectfully as I enter. I give her and the others a quick nod, then stand aside, watching but not intervening. I see her lip curve in a smile as she nods back; when men are present, she wears the hijab but not the full veil, as is customary where she was born. For a moment I recall the scent of Ahava's hair and the sensation of it against my chest, but I take a breath and banish the memory.

"All is ready?" I ask.

Malala stands, her gaze fixed respectfully on a point just

below my eyes. "Allah has made us ready."

"It is well."

Her eyes are fierce with pride. She has earned that pride. She and her team are the best we have ever sent. And that is needed. Because this time, I am not sending the team to greet some alien species across the expanse of years.

I am sending them to greet *us*.

Six days ago, the psichartography lab identified a unique psionic signature from the vicinity of a dwarf star on the other side of Darb Al-Tabanah. I received the call immediately. We had been looking for this, waiting for this. For years.

They had found a human signature.

Our descendants are *out there*.

I've made sure the Ansible 15715 team knows the bodies they are transferring to are human, but they haven't been told that they are crossing a gap of generations and not only space. Nor that whatever minds currently function within those new bodies may not survive the Ansible team's sudden occupation of them—something I have long forbid myself to think about; it is terribly possible that our future and our freedom from the violence of the past can be bought only with more violence. I will not share the responsibility for that.

I want no squeamishness on this team.

Facing them, I recite the words that have become ritual because I have said them so many times before. "Allah alone knows if we will speak again, you and I, but know that your names will be written in the plinths outside. And on my heart, and on the hearts of all the Faithful. Where you are going, none of the Faithful have ever been. Be wise. Be methodical. Be strong of heart. *Fi amanillah.*"

"*Ma salaam,*" they murmur back.

Malala signals with her hand, and the others file out the other door, headed up to the gardens. The safer gardens, the smaller ones with no bodies in them. Malala remains behind a moment.

"You want to say something, Ansible?"

Her shoulders are stiff. I watch her take a quick breath. "Thank you, President," she says quickly. "For choosing us. For training us. Thank you."

Her jawline is tight with emotion. I suppress an urge to look away, to hide my own face—though her gaze is still lowered and respectful. If Ahava had thanked me before going, I would not have survived it. At least I have the small consolation of knowing that I fought her, that what happened to her was against my will, though no less my fault.

Not so with these young ones.

My throat is closed and I cannot speak. I just nod. She must have seen the motion, because she nods back and then turns and steps briskly from the room. In another moment, the room is only an empty box with white walls and a white ceiling and sleek metal devices discarded on low tables like unneeded memories. And I am alone there.

I stand gazing down at the missives. I even touch one, trailing my fingertips across its surface, still warm from another hand. Unsure why I am tormenting myself. None of these missives will make it to the families, of course. If Starmind is to take the risks we must, then there can be little knowledge outside of anything that happens here. I should leave the missives here to be discarded safely by the staff, but on a sudden impulse I begin gathering them all up, piling them awkwardly in the crook of my left arm.

Stepping outside with them, I catch a glimpse of two of our psionic medics. I nod to them and step by quickly. Maybe they will not be needed.

This time, it might work.

It might.

We are trying a new equation, a new adjustment. We might retain contact once the Ansibles are out there. We might receive messages from across time.

Think what we might learn from our children, what our grandfathers might have learned from *us* if they only could have. This is how we will restore a green and lawful world—by the wisdom of our daughters and sons.

That is worth the sacrifices I have made.

I must tell myself that.

***

I am not watching when Malala's team transfers out. I never watch, now. There is no cup of coffee in my hand. I lay on my bed with my eyes closed. A tap of my fingers behind my left ear wakens the implant there, and my dark world fills with music. A blink of my eye tells the implant to skip from one composition to the next. I blink through them quickly: a woman singing a Hindi love song, an aria from a decadent European opera from centuries past, a Nigerian chant, and finally the quiet plucking of strings on a kacapi, like the one my grandfather used to play on his balcony overlooking the dead but still restless sea.

An old man's raspy yet deep vocal accompanies the kacapi, and I realize that I am translating his words from Malay to Arabic in my head, as I have done most of my adult life. I stop and just listen in my childhood language. It is a song my grandfather would have liked: sad and wistful yet with a sort of deep bravado to it, too. *Where the whales, where have the whales gone, all the whales, oh, oh, all the mighty whales in the sea, I will call them back, all of them back, if I sing only loudly, loudly enough...*

I sigh and lift my hands to my head, rubbing my temples. Fantasies. The sea is still dead. I am chasing dreams like an unbearded youth drunk on his first sight of a dancing girl. Somewhere in the long walk of years I have imbibed too deeply of the Old Man's drugs, and now I stagger across the desert, knife in hand or scalpel, leaving bodies behind me as I search for a paradise that is only a shimmer of imagined water on the desert air. The pages of the Quran flutter in the dry wind, and the neural monitors beep and ping in the quiet of the labs, and none of us are any closer. We are just putting off dying of thirst on the sands.

Getting up and swinging my feet off the bed, I sit in the darkened room, listening to that kacapi. Something I have done or will do, will work. I know this, because out in that wide future we have detected human minds on worlds other than our own. On some future day that I can't see, the mirage becomes real.

I am not ready to leave the room yet, and no one will page me or disturb me until I am ready. I don't allow any communications equipment in my room. This is a place for peace and prayer, and for the privacy of my night terrors. Business is for outside the door.

Stooping, I collect one of the missives from the floor. My hand trembles as I hold it; with a flash of anger at myself, I punch in and start the recording. I haven't silenced my own implant, so the kacapi offers a quiet, eerie score to a young man's last words to his mother and father. He is speaking a Swahili dialect that I do not know, but the emotion is plain. There is a quiver in his voice, but it is excitement. In his heart he has already sent the message; he is thinking only of the joy of being in a new place, in a new body, among new and barely comprehensible people, breathing new air beneath a new sun.

The next missive is sorrowful as though the young woman stands at her daughter's grave. It is not Malala's voice. Hasna, I think. These words are Arabic, and I can hear her demanding of her daughter a promise that she will go to KAUST and achieve a degree and start a career before she finds a good Arab boy to marry. These missives piled on my carpet are now relics of lost lives. I should establish some tradition here of treasuring them up, of holding them sacred, for these are the lives and loves of men and women who bear the words of Mohammad and my own wish for peace out beyond the nearer stars. Surely they are each deserving of more honor than any camel archer or warlike emissary of centuries past who crossed mere earthly deserts. I should make some new tradition. I will, before nightfall. I will think of something, and I will do it, and we will go on doing it each time an Ansible team does not report back.

***

"I have never been so excited," Malala's voice says near my ear, "nor so terrified. Sister, I am about to see things no one has ever seen, no one has ever imagined. If you were here now I would kiss you and sob into your hair, but how can I even sound sad on this? Allah, Allah, I will miss you. But the things I am going to *see* and *do*." And a choked sound like a sob. "I am going to *miss* you! You are in my heart, Noushin, you are in my heart."

Then the quiet, barely perceptible click of the recording's end, and Malala is gone, and the new song against the bone behind my ear is an ancestral battle song torn from the strings of the kacapi – violence translated into music. I tap my head quickly, cutting it off.

My breathing comes heavily. A glance at the chronom on the wall warns me, and I kneel facing Mecca, bending my brow to the carpet. The words of prayer come swiftly to my lips, but I find it hard to quiet and submit my heart. Malala's voice is in my head, in the bones of my head. Such eagerness, like a child handed an as-yet-unopened gift. And she *is* young, they are all so young, and I have grown old—when did I grow old? I am sending children away to die. Summoning them here from nations around the globe, then losing them in the heart of my own labyrinth. Not the architect, I, but the power-hungry caliph. If I only knew what monster is harbored at the labyrinth's deepest point, or how it might be slain, or what golden thread might lead the children—and my own wife—out again.

***

While we were still freshly wed, Ahava and I visited the ruin of Iguaza Falls, where not even a trickle of water remains. She stood staring at that dry drop for an hour without speaking. Then, after evening prayer, she raved with the dying sun in her hair. "I could kill the people who did this," she said. "I could kill them." She had fire in her eyes and fire in her heart, and I had never yet heard her speak so passionately as she did then at dusk. I think Iguaza was a great shock to her. She had grown from girl to woman in an offshore arcology, not in the open air like me. All her life the affluence of her family had sheltered her from sights like these. When I showed her the trash fields in the Atlantic, she wept.

We shared the same nightmare, after that, and the same dream. So I believed. It was Ahava who designed the training for the Ansibles, who took us from transferring the minds of mice to those of Allah's own people. We still use her techniques at Starmind; the rigors of psionic discipline here are hers.

She drew so close to those first Ansibles; one even left her last missive to Ahava, as though making a farewell to a beloved mother. Yet I refused Ahava access to the gardens from which the Ansibles transferred, refused to let her see any of the psionic readings, refused to tell her of their mouths locked open in silent shrieks. Then she began training as a member of the second team herself. Maybe because she trusted me, maybe because she didn't, and she meant only to force the truth from me. She had designed the training; it was her area of authority here at Starmind. To keep her from it might have shattered her love for me.

A coward, I stood outside the sensory deprivation tanks while she practiced psicasting, brushing remote places with her mind. I worked the gymnasium with her, admiring the lithe strength of her body as I did so often in our bed. By night, I consoled myself deep inside her and tried never to think of Ansible 1; by day, I watched her prepare for her death. I could have told her. I could have saved her. I had only to abandon everything else, everything else to the wind.

***

"Salaam." I open the com.

"Salaam."

"Did they transfer?"

"They transferred." Barely repressed excitement in the younger man's voice. Something wakens in me, hearing it. I hold my breath.

"They did, President," the medic tells me. "Something is…is different, President."

***

I am there in less than four minutes. They have her spread out across a table and I can see the gentle rise and fall of her breast. Her eyes are open but her mouth is not; there is no silent scream in Malala's face.

Now my eyes are moist, at last, after all these years. I sniff and lean over the woman, making the others in the lab a little uncomfortable. I do not care. Allah only will judge my actions.

"She made it through," one of the medics says, as though it *must* be said, his voice in that hush one uses when stepping into a mosque.

"Readings?" I whisper, not taking my eyes from the Iranian's face.

My mind catalogues pulse, temperature, psichiometry, adrenaline, norepinepherine, and exactly twenty-seven other critical indicators. But I am watching her eyes, awaiting some message, some signal.

"Nothing on psi," the medic tells me.

"But the link is stable?"

"Yes."

"You're certain?"

"It's stable." The man's voice has calmed, perhaps from his own litany of medical and psionic readings.

"So our end of the link is silent," I murmur, "but we may hope that she is alive and sane." I glance at the stretchers that arrived just before I ran in, at the twitching bodies belted to them. "Not the others, but *she* made it through." I gesture to the tech with my hand. "Send the modulation she used to every lab, every team. From this day, we use that one and that one only."

"Already done."

"Why are her eyes dilated? I have never seen that happen before—not in the mice—"

"We don't know."

I tap behind my ear, and my head fills again with the strings of the kacapi. I want to remember this moment. I want to remember it every time I hear that music, I want that kacapi to call it back to me on every night that I wake sweating at the sounds of a woman's fingernails against glass. This moment will be my shield and my dome lifted in praise of he who is All Compassionate and who drops universes from his hand the way a jeweler drops diamonds onto a dark fabric, to show them off as things of unparalleled and indescribable beauty. For an instant I recall the first time I kissed Ahava and felt her lips so lovely against my own. The soft joy in her eyes when she pulled back. "What is that I see in your eyes?" she whispered to me.

"Hope," I whispered back. "Hope." And I kissed her again.

That was many years ago. But she would see it in my eyes now. Hope. And a brightness of stars above me.

"Have Musa brought here. And get Zakir to send the next two teams. Immediately." I can barely hear my own words.

"We need time to test her, President, to watch—"

"We have already burned years behind us like cities on fire," I reply. "Send them *now*. And double shifts for the deprivation tanks. I want eight more teams ready to go before Ramadan."

"If something goes wrong—"

But I have stopped listening. Already I am calculating

who else I can send to that planet, to our descendants. The rest of the teams that are nearly ready now must go to the worlds and species for which they are already targeted and conditioned. But I need to send more *out there* where Malala Ali has gone. I need to get a link that can communicate back.

***

She is monitored night and day, and the weeks swoop past like the owls that live now only in carefully designed refuges—I have seen them often—but that once lived in the night air and in the high rocks, in every crevasse of our world. I can hear the owl-screech of the weeks in my ears and the numbers on the chronom spin by so fast I can hardly read them. Like Mohammad's camel-mounted emissaries, we charge into the future. I fling Ansible after Ansible across the dark, and now I no longer retreat to my room. In fact I am never there anymore, only to sleep. I don't stand still except to pray. I still visit Ahava each morning, but now I pace about her cryotube, manic, almost frantic, describing to her the worlds to which I have thrown the young men and women, the worlds and the strange minds on those worlds, and I talk very fast, as though I am Shahrazad and she the sultan on the edge of sleep, and I must keep her wakeful and listening to my stories lest she slumber and then pass sentence in the morning.

I watch each of the teams transfer out now, and watch

their breathing and watch their faces and listen to the quiet noises of psionic and medical and neurological monitors afterward. Not all of them make it, but most do. And there are still no messages back. Neither their faces nor their minds share with us any hint of the people they encounter, the conversations they have, the joys or the miseries they endure.

But they live.

And I stand here waiting on the ashes of earth, ignoring all missives that come in from king or ayatollah or from any of the republics or oligarchies or colonies of Dar al-Islam. I ignore them all. There is no longer time to answer; I can't be distracted by politics or demands for accountability from those who have sanctioned a project they barely understand. I listen only to the nostalgic cry of the kacapi. *The whales, oh, oh, all the mighty whales.* What whales swim out in that eternal dark that Allah has chosen in his goodness to light with ten billion billion points of fire? What tents already or soon to be pitched on planets whose skies rain water like ours, or acid like Venus's, or diamonds like Neptune's, or liquid methane, or other rains still more alien and more strange—what tents will later shelter us or send their goods and knowledge to reprieve us? What stick will some alien god or some distant as-yet-unnamed granddaughter hand us that will strike water from the rock of our desert earth, like Moses's stick in Ahava's favorite story? I am like a boy on the edge of a lake with a mountain of pebbles, and I am throwing in rocks with both hands, dozens at a time, spreading them far, waiting for fish ancient and fat to rise to the surface, their eyes wide and unblinking with wisdom. I will throw in more Ansibles, more Ansibles, I will empty the nations if I must, every man or woman who can touch another mind will go to touch these that we have found, human or alien, all these other minds waiting for us out in that immensity. I will make the surface of that lake into froth. And whatever lives in the deep with Allah will answer. I will not let it rest until it does. It must answer me. All of you out there in that dark, I am Abdullah Takwan, born in New Penang on China's Broken Shore, degreed in drowned Jakarta and New Jeddah; I am the apostle who has destroyed children and damned my own wife and who will save a world. My mind has touched the stars, wearing a thousand faces, and you will answer.

Any day now, any day.

ANSIBLE WILL CONTINUE IN SEASON TWO
WITH "ANSIBLE 15718"

ACKNOWLEDGMENTS

In bringing you these stories, I owe a debt to my early readers—Teddi Deppner, Christy Spry, Mike Long, Sue Hildinger Hoerner, Jason Kirk, and Allison M. Dickson—and to the writers at Westmarch Publishing, fine people all. You all inspire me and encourage me! And I owe much to my patrons at Patreon, who have been there beside in the making of some extravagant projects! And, most especially, I am grateful to my wife Jessica and to my two little ones, River and Inara, without whose fire and laughter I would probably never get any fiction finished at all; you three are my heart.

DID YOU ENJOY THESE STORIES?

If yes, consider joining my Patreon membership: http://www.patreon.com/stantlitore

I use Patreon to fund my independent work and to make it possible for my fiction to support the needs of my disabled, three-year-old daughter Inara. You can learn more at my Patreon page—and if you join as one of my members there, I will send you ebooks!

You can also reach me at zombiebible@gmail.com. I look forward to hearing what you thought of the story!

Stant Litore

ABOUT STANT LITORE

Stant Litore is the author of the *Ansible* stories and *The Zombie Bible*. He has an intense love of ancient languages, a fierce admiration for his ancestors, and a fascination with religion and history. He doesn't consider his writing a vocation; he considers it an act of survival. Litore lives in Colorado with his wife and two daughters and is at work on his next book.

You can learn more about Litore's work at:
www.stantlitore.com.

CPSIA information can be obtained
at www.ICGtesting.com
Printed in the USA
LVOW07s0046100118
562510LV00001B/33/P